Mr. Putter & Tabby
Clear the Decks

CYNTHIA RYLANT

Mr. Putter & Tabby
Clear the Decks

Illustrated by

ARTHUR HOWARD

Harcourt Children's Books

Houghton Mifflin Harcourt   Boston   New York   2010

For my friends
Patrick and Janie

—C.R.

For my dad
—A.H.

Text copyright © 2010 by Cynthia Rylant
Illustrations copyright © 2010 by Arthur Howard

Harcourt Children's Books is an imprint of
Houghton Mifflin Harcourt Publishing Company.

www.hmhbooks.com

The illustrations in this book were done in pencil, watercolor,
and gouache on 250-gram cotton rag paper.
The text type was set in Berkeley Old Style Book.
The display type was set in Minya Nouvelle, Agenda, and Artcraft.

Library of Congress Cataloging-in-Publication Data
Rylant, Cynthia.
Mr. Putter & Tabby clear the decks / Cynthia Rylant ;
illustrated by Arthur Howard.
p.   cm.
Summary: During a long, hot summer, fun-loving neighbor Mrs. Teaberry
and her mischievous dog, Zeke, take a bored Mr. Putter and his cat, Tabby,
on an adventurous sightseeing boat cruise.
ISBN 978-0-15-206715-1 (hardcover : alk. paper)
[1. Old age—Fiction.   2. Neighbors—Fiction.   3. Cats—Fiction.   4. Boats
and boating—Fiction.   5. Summer—Fiction.]   I. Howard, Arthur, ill.
II. Title.   III. Title: Mr. Putter and Tabby clear the decks.
IV. Title: Mister Putter & Tabby clear the decks.
PZ7.R982Mscg 2010
[E]—dc22   2009036670

Manufactured in China
LEO 1 3 5 7 9 10 8 6 4 2
4500223861

1

Itchy

It was summer, and Mr. Putter
and his fine cat, Tabby, were itchy.
They were not itchy because of fleas.
There was *never* a flea in Mr. Putter's house!
They were itchy because they were bored.

The days had become hot and long.
It seemed that all they did was lie around
and dream of orangesicles.

They needed some adventure.
And Mr. Putter always knew
where adventure was.
It was next door.

2

An Idea

Mrs. Teaberry lived next door.
She lived next door with her
good dog, Zeke, and they were
very adventurous.

They took adventurous classes, like diving.

They ate adventurous food, like squid.
And they *loved* adventurous movies.
They watched those all the time.

So Mr. Putter called Mrs. Teaberry.

"Tabby and I are itchy," said Mr. Putter.

"Oh, dear," said Mrs. Teaberry.

"Perhaps you need a flea bath."

"No, no," said Mr. Putter. "We are bored.
It is hot, the days are long,
and we have no orangesicles."
"You need an adventure," said Mrs. Teaberry.
"I have an idea."

Mr. Putter was glad.

Sort of glad.

Mrs. Teaberry's ideas sometimes took him

to strange places.

3

Pepping Up

Mrs. Teaberry and Zeke showed up
at Mr. Putter's door.
They had sunblock, sunglasses,
and sun hats.

"Are we going in the sun?" asked Mr. Putter.
He was already so hot.
More sun did not sound like fun.
"Don't worry," said Mrs. Teaberry. "We are
going on a boat. A sightseeing boat."

Mr. Putter pepped up.

"A sightseeing boat?" he said. "I *love* sightseeing!"

"I know," said Mrs. Teaberry with a smile.

Sometimes Mrs. Teaberry was a genius.

4

A Boat!

The sightseeing boat was named *The Olden Days*.
Mr. Putter liked it right away
because he and Tabby were both old.
They liked being old.
Mr. Putter was glad the boat was not named
The Young and Zippy Days.
Those were long behind him.

Mr. Putter and Tabby and Mrs. Teaberry and Zeke
stood at the very front of the bow.
The wind blew in their faces.
The gulls flew by.
They felt free.
FREE!

"Free orangesicles!" called the captain.

Mr. Putter looked at Mrs. Teaberry.

"You are a genius," said Mr. Putter.

Mrs. Teaberry smiled.

5

Another Boat!

At the end of the day, the sightseeing cruise was over.

Mr. Putter and Mrs. Teaberry and Tabby were ready to go home.

But Zeke was not ready.

He loved *The Olden Days*.

He loved the wind and the water.

Plus everyone kept feeding him french fries.

Zeke did not want to go home.

He clamped his teeth on a mast.

Zeke would not let go.

Mr. Putter tugged.

Mrs. Teaberry tugged.

Zeke would *not* let go.

Then the captain came along.
The captain knew what it was like
to love a boat.
He knew how to talk to Zeke.
He sat down and told Zeke
many things.
Zeke listened.

Then the captain pulled a dog toy
from his pocket.
It looked like a boat.
To take the boat, Zeke would have to
let go of the mast.

Zeke wanted the boat.

He let go of the mast.

"HOORAY!" everyone said.

They all went home happy.

Mr. Putter and Tabby took a nap.

Mrs. Teaberry took a bath.

And Zeke sailed his boat!